THE RIDING MAN

A Novella

By

Earl Griffin

INFINITY
PUBLISHING.COM

ISBN 0-7414-5479-3

Front cover: Original artwork by Norene Cline

Published by:

PUBLISHING.COM

*1094 New DeHaven Street, Suite 100
West Conshohocken, PA 19428-2713
Info@buybooksontheweb.com
www.buybooksontheweb.com
Toll-free (877) BUY BOOK
Local Phone (610) 941-9999
Fax (610) 941-9959*

Printed in the United States of America

Published June 2009

To Richard:

Too often I have lived my life

And forfeited living my love.

You never have!

Foreword

The conversations came as quixotic as the snow and ice that winter. For days, mile after silent mile on horseback, as the agony of the unaccustomed exertion cut into my thighs and lower back, we rode through the harshest winter since '47 when a blizzard brought such a snow that vehicles were paralyzed in place as late as the fourteenth day of April. Silently we loped a thousand miles mostly within the confines of the timbered round pen, sometimes down the sandy road to the Home Place and twice dangerously down the river searching for storm stranded cattle. And with each silent horse bound mile I struggled to either create conversation between us or force them upon him. Then, without warning, invitation or reason, they would come to us.

But Richard's conversation was not conversation as most know it. His was a conversation of listening, not speaking; listening to the gait of the roan filly to learn if she dropped her front right ankle when she began her trot, still yielding to the pain of a misstep into a badger's hole earlier in the fall; listening to the paint's breathing to see if any remnant of the near fatal pneumonia still hid within his lungs; listening with the palm of his hand to the bay's bowel sounds to be certain his colic had not become chronic.

And I could not yet hear this silent speak of horses and of the very few who still could, the remnants of a time when a horse was life amidst these short grass prairies and only those who could truly know a horse could survive here. I strained to have Richard explain to me these haunting sounds he heard and I could not hear. He refused to even try.

But through the miles we rode together I have learned to hear these sounds. And I have learned Richard knew I would learn and knew I could only learn by listening to them for myself and not through his or anyone else's explanation of them.

So I ride and I wait and I listen because I must if I am to have these conversations with Richard which I desperately seek. And as I begin to learn to listen the conversations come. Many of them are only quick bursts of guttural sounds. Some are a few lines of comic relief. A few, a very precious few, help me to learn to listen, to learn that in listening there is meaning, even to lost loves, broken dreams and fickle chance, to learn that for the seers, the Shamans and the real cowboys that by listening they live and that life is the thing they listen to.

Listen.

1.

"Shit! What happened?" I cursed. I rolled onto my side and rose to my knees in the loose sand of the round pen. "Did the damn horse throw me?"

Richard sat on his horse, holding the black filly's reins, rubbing her between her ears and staring into her soft brown eyes. He sat, rubbed and stared.

"Well?" I demanded.

Richard sighed, rubbed the filly between her ears one more time and said. "Well. 'looked to me more like you fell off the horse than the horse threw you off."

Richard slipped the bridle across the filly's ears and freed the snaffle bit from her mouth. He let the bridle drop to the ground. He had his right arm draped around the black filly's neck and he held a blue halter in his left hand. He slid the bottom loop of the halter across her nose. He eased the top loop over her ears and tied the halter together behind her left ear. He snapped the catch on the end of a lead rope into the ring on the halter and led the filly out of the round pen as I limped behind.

"If you tie her off she'll just break the lead rope." I warned.

"We're going to deal with that now." Richard said.

He dropped the heavy coils of the unusually long lead rope onto the hard packed dirt of the alley between the stalls. He tied the other end of the lead rope securely to one of the hitching rings which were attached to the pylons which supported the roof of the half-barn.

The black filly sat back hard expecting the lead rope to hold her. It did not. It uncoiled. She almost fell upon her rear haunches. The black filly staggered upright, twitched her ears and sat back again, but this time not as hard as she had the first time. The rope uncoiled some more and the black stumbled again. She stopped, stood a moment, backed up a step or two and stopped. She saw she was still tied to the ring. But backing away did nothing to free her. She stood.

"Few more times on that long lead and she'll quit setting back and breaking reins when you tie her." Richard said. He reached down and picked up a stiff bristled brush and tossed it to me. "Helps to be smarter than the horse." He chuckled and said. "Brush her off after you unsaddle her."

I brushed the last flakes of dust off of the black filly's coat. "Don't know why I'm brushing this damn horse." I grumbled and tossed the brush into the wooden carpenter's box used to store the brushes and curry combs.

"'have to." Richard said.

4

"Why do I have to?"

"If you leave her sweaty and dusty after riding her, that is what she remembers. That following a ride she will be hot and dusty and uncomfortable." Richard picked up the brush and completed cleaning the black's back.

"I'm going to Amarillo tomorrow." I said.

"Why?"

"I'm still trying to find that book I told you about."

"'didn't find it last time?"

"No." I said. "Maybe Barnes and Nobles will have it this time."

"To that waste disposal group again?" Richard asked. He laid the brush in the wooden box and led the filly to her stall.

I waited for him to explain what he meant about the bookstore. Waiting for Richard to explain was like waiting for rain in West Texas. It would come. It always did. But it always takes its time and never comes when you most want it. I gave up. "Anything you need from Amarillo?" I asked.

"'can't think of anything I've left there that I need." Richard climbed up into the travel trailer parked underneath the metal barn. I left.

2.

I led the black from her stall and tied her to the outside rail of the round pen where I had dropped a saddle blanket and Boss' saddle.

Richard approached from within the barn.

I picked up the thick woolen saddle blanket from where I had dropped it.

Richard frowned, stepped between me and the black filly and brushed her withers beneath the end of her mane. "You have to get all the dust, residue and all, gone. Otherwise, the blanket will cause it to chafe against her back and cause a hot spot." Richard instructed me.

"So I brush her before I ride her. I brush her after I ride her. I pay each ninety days to have her shod. I feed her twice a day. I shovel her shit once a day. And she deposits my ass on top of a prickly pear stand anytime she chooses."

"That's about how it works." Richard curried the black's back with the side of his rough hands which were interchanged with deep cracks that seemed to descend like bottomless crevasses and hard-panned calluses. "'horse's well-being is what is important."

I shook my head. Richard took the saddle blanket from me and laid it across the black. He gripped the horn on the old saddle and hesitated. He studied the saddle.

I looked at the saddle. It was one of the last Fort Worth's famed saddle makers, M. L. Leddy, had built. It was as good a saddle as E. L. 'Shorty' Mullins could buy for his last son. The son for whom he had taken all of the too few veteran dollars he had received for running messages between the Allied trenches of the Somme during World War I to carry to doctor after doctor seeking to free the little boy of the down syndrome which plagued the boy's growth, the boy's speech and Shorty Mullins' heart and soul.

Each doctor told Shorty that his boy would never go to school, would never be able to learn to read or write. But Shorty Mullins refused to hear the first one or the second one and on, until by the tenth one he no longer possessed any money to carry his boy to yet another doctor. All ten of the doctors told Shorty to take his boy home, to keep the boy there as long as he could, hopefully until the boy died which would probably be before he became a teenager.

Shorty Mullins had cursed the doctors and then he had taken his son home. But he did not take the boy home just to wait and watch him die. Shorty taught his son what Shorty knew best. He taught him about horses and how to ride them. And the boy that could not learn learned to ride as no horseman then alive on the short grass prairie could ride, to ride as well as legend claimed the horse cultured Comanche had ridden.

Shorty Mullins' Boss Man was a horseman. And because he was Shorty Mullins was determined this would mean something.

What it meant was that Boss rode the best horse careful breeding could coax from the group of brood mares Shorty kept to be bred to the best studs he could find. It meant Boss had the best horse that hour upon hour upon hour of late night training, until both man and horse staggered from fatigue, could create; the best horse for his Boss Man which Shorty Mullins' iron will could draw from the long sinewy sorrel colt which Boss called Major. The best horse the old horseman could hone from muscle, blood and more---from his and the sorrel's spirit.

The training ceased only when Shorty knew that the sorrel knew that its entire purpose in being was to serve the boy man Shorty helped into the saddle on its back, to carry that boy man upright on his saddle across a storm angered White's Creek while more experienced riders slid from their saddles and prayed that their shying mounts would swim to the far side of the creek through the sliding mud and swelling rise of its flood, to stand resolute and still amidst the riot of car horn spooked horses in parade after parade from the rugged rodeo grounds at Roaring Springs to the refinement of the Will Rogers Coliseum in Fort Worth, and to nuzzle the sloped shoulders of the short boy man who cursed him lovingly in an unknown tongue.

It meant acceptance for Shorty's Boss Man, and respect and dignity all the days of Boss' long life.

Elmer Leland 'Shorty' Mullins and Oma Faye 'Big Mud' Mullins had taken the last of their four children home. Not to die by ten or twelve or surely fourteen as the doctors had predicted, but to live. And live he did by riding on the best saddles and the best horses Shorty and Big Mud could get for him.

It took a massive stroke to take the old horseman, Shorty Mullins, before his youngest son had left this world.

Nothing could take 'Big Mud' before her boy. She struggled passed her ninety-sixth year to survive by six months her youngest child who died after his sixty-second birthday.

Boss' saddle carried more than just sweaty butts. It carried dignity and respect and horsemen. It carried the past.

I watched Richard remember that past as he hesitated before he lifted it off of the ground and slid it across the black's back. He tightened the cinch with two slight tugs, looped the latigo through the stainless steel ring on the saddle but he did not lock the pin into one of the holes in the latigo.

Richard saw me notice that he had not fastened the latigo into the saddle ring. "With these young horses don't try to fasten the cinch on the first pulls. Wait a few minutes then pull the cinch again and fasten it." Richard said.

"Why?"

"Because these young horses react to the cinch. They are not used to it. So they hold their breath. You tighten the cinch on the first pulls and mount, then they relax and," Richard shrugged.

"And you're sitting on a loose saddle on a green horse and they blow up and you end up hanging in a saddle underneath their belly with them going insane."

Richard massaged his dip against his bottom lip. "Can happen." He said. The black let out her breath. Richard pulled the cinch tight and fastened the catch pen into a hole in the latigo. "Know why the saddle ring is stainless steel?"

"No."

"Steel rusts. Horses sweat most beneath the saddle and the sweat gathers along the cinch and latigo. Latigo carries the sweat to the saddle ring. Rusted saddle ring cuts the latigo and," Richard spit.

"And again you have a loose saddle." I finished Richard's insight for him.

Richard nodded. "Loose saddle has hurt many a cowboy."

I smiled and sighed. "A loose saddle hurts many people in many different situations."

Richard handed me the black's reins. I led her to the round pen for more ground work.

"What time did you get back from Amarillo last night?" Richard asked.

"After ten." I answered. "I spent a couple of hours looking for my book."

"Find it?"

I shook my head. "No. Barnes And Nobles still doesn't carry it."

Richard pulled his dip from his lip and flicked it on the ground. "Damn waste disposal group." He spit the dip's leavings.

3.

Richard pitched forked clumps of the sweet alfalfa into one of the round plastic tubs which twice a day he used to feed the horses. He had arranged the tubs in a semi-circle before the hay bin.

"What can I do?" I asked.

Richard shoved the pitchfork into the alfalfa, picked up an eight fingered manure rake, laid it in the rusted wheelbarrow and slid the wheelbarrow toward me. "Muck the stalls."

I looked at the dozen stalls. Green manure layered with late season flies steamed in all of them. "Which one do I start with?" I asked. I gripped the wheelbarrow's wooden handles and lifted the back of the barrel off of the ground.

"Suit yourself." Richard said and resumed forking alfalfa into the tubs.

An hour later I laid the manure rake on top of the third wheelbarrow full of manure, wrestled the wheelbarrow through the gate of the black filly's stall, latched the gate behind me and wiped the sweat from my face with my sleeve. Plop. Plop. Plop. Three new stacks of manure sizzled beneath the black filly's swishing tail. The filly watched me through big soft doe eyes. I shook my head.

Richard laughed as he opened the gate to her stall. "Hand me the manure rake."

I handed him the rake. He scooped the fresh manure from the ground, carried it to the wheelbarrow and slapped the wet manure on to the pile.

"She do that on purpose?" I asked.

"Probably." Richard lifted the wheelbarrow's handles. "I'll dump this load for you."

Richard leaned the empty wheelbarrow on its nose and against the first stall and said, "'saddle Aztec."

"What for?"

"You forgot?"

"'guess I did."

"We're gonna' pen the cattle at the river and sort the keeper heifers. 'bring them back here and pen 'em. I'll use 'em to train the horses until next spring. Then we can put the black bull with them." Richard reminded me.

"That's right. You said we were going to sort keeper heifers today." I nodded. I looked at the black filly.

Richard shook his head. "Not yet. She's not ready to work cattle outside." Richard said. "And you're not ready to work cattle on a green horse."

I frowned. But I picked up a halter and walked to the far outside stall where Richard kept the two old geldings, Sammy, a paint with one sky blue eye and one brown eye, and Aztec, a large black gelding. Both horses had spent fifteen years under Richard's saddle running winter wheat steers for the Dripping Springs, JA's and other large ranches above the Caprock.

I led Aztec to the tack room.

Richard swung two blankets up onto Aztec's back. Aztec put his ears forward and turned his face to Richard. Richard patted his neck. "Time to go to work again, old man." Richard said and scratched the horse beneath his long jaw. He pulled the blankets forward and high on to Aztec's shoulders and said to me. "Throw Boss' saddle up on him. 'let's see how much we have to let the buck cinch out to fasten it around his middle."

It took the last notch in the buck cinch to span Aztec's belly. Richard laughed. "Damn! He needs some hard ridin'." He handed the snaffle bit's reins to me. "'best take him to the round pen. 'step up on him there. He's plenty gentle. But he hasn't been ridden so long 'old fool might just try you."

I struggled up into Boss' saddle. Richard stood beside the young red roan he was training and watched Aztec trot three circles around the round pen. "He's good." Richard said. I eased the gelding to the center of the round pen and watched Richard put the red roan through several twisting figure eights. Richard nodded. I leaned down and pulled the spring held handle and freed the round bar from its seat in the slot cut into the pipe standard of the round pen. Richard and I rode to the road and turned north to the river place.

The cattle milled in the upper corral above the windmill and the smaller lower corral. Richard moved the red roan among them, single reining him around mother cows to edge any female calf above four hundred pounds from their sides and force them passed Aztec and me as we blocked the open gate leading to the lower pen. A dozen bawling heifer calves eyed Aztec's rear legs for a route back into the upper pen where their mothers bawled for them to return.

"If I can get that last big red heifer away from Old Fight, we will close the gate on 'em and be done." Richard said. He touched the red roan with his spurs and aimed him at Old Fight and her red heifer calf.

Old Fight was well named. As a heifer with her first calf she had knocked the captain through a wooden gate when he had ventured close to her calf. Fortunately for the captain the dry rotted gate shattered and he had rolled free of the attack without anything injured other than his dignity. "Damned old fightin' fool!" The captain had cursed. Thus, Old Fight she became and stayed. She would fight man, horse or beast to keep her calves safe at her side. And she had kept eleven calves safe.

"Watch her." I warned as Richard approached Old Fight and her calf.

Richard tried to rein the red roan around the rear of Old Fight. But the red roan seemed mesmerized by the glare glowing in Old Fight's yellow eyes. He ignored the rein and stepped in front of the cow. Old Fight saw her opportunity. She charged the red roan which now stood broadside to her and stared at her. She took the red roan on his shoulder with her chest and drove him sideways. As she did she slung her battered horns at Richard, missed him, but hooked the reins and tore them from his grip. Richard sat rudderless before a snot slinging bellowing battleship which was gathering itself to ram the roan horse amidships. If she hit the red roan now as he staggered, trying to regain his footing, she would send him crashing onto his side and he would pen Richard's once broken leg beneath the horse and saddle and possibly roll the horse over the top of Richard.

I watched, frozen, spellbound by Old Fight's fury and agility. Aztec did not. He bolted forward, his ears back. The great black horse chortled his own fury at Old Fight. Aztec drove his chest into Old Fight's shoulder.

Old Fight staggered sideways, smashing her crying calf against the working chute. The calf stumbled away from its mother. Old Fight turned to rejoin her calf, giving up her attack on Richard and the red roan.

Aztec wheeled between Old Fight and the calf, preventing the mother from reclaiming her calf. The big horse reached forward and bit the calf on its hip. The calf screamed with hurt and fear and ran from the large horse. Aztec raced between the calf and the gathered herd of cattle at the top of the pen. He forced the calf through the gate and into the lower pen with the other calves, wheeled around blocking the calves return to the upper pen with his hindquarters and eliminating the mothers' hopes of regaining their offspring for not even Old Fight would challenge the great black horse now.

Richard eased the red roan up to Aztec. Aztec raised his head high. The red roan lowered his in submission and Aztec lowered his head and rubbed his jaw along the younger horse's mane. "That was one hell of a move." Richard said. "You saved my ass."

"I swear, Richard." I said. "All I did was hang on for dear life. He did it all on his own." I nodded at the horse on which I sat.

Richard reached and rubbed Aztec's cheek. "Young horse is stronger, quicker. But this old man." He fingered Aztec's ear. "He's been through all the wrecks. He can see 'em comin' and he's still fearless." Richard looked at me. "'young horse will wreck you more often than not. Unless there is an old wise head around to save you." He stroked Aztec's cheek one more time. "Thanks old man." He said before he rested his hands on his saddle's horn.

4.

Faint light drew a thin line along the eastern horizon. I yawned and stretched and continued brushing the black filly's back. Richard laced the saddled red roan's lead rope into the tie ring next to the one the black filly was tied to. He picked up the soft wool blanket and laid it across the black's back, picked up the thicker saddle pad and laid it atop the blanket. I tossed the brush into the grooming bucket and lifted Boss' saddle off of the ground and swung it atop the pad. Richard pushed the cinch to me underneath the black. "Cinch her easy for now." He instructed me. "We'll warm 'em up in the round pen before we head for the river. Then you can tighten her cinch down."

Today I would ride the black filly outside of the round pen for the first time. I reached forward with my left spur and touched her shoulder as I lifted both reins with my left hand and moved my hand to the left. The loping filly turned easily, responding to both the reins and my spur. Still loping she swung out into the round pen. I continued to rein her around to the left, but I released the pressure of my spur. I took her back along the same track and made two circuits of the round pen. I reached with my right spur, caught her in front of her right shoulder, separated the reins in my hands and extended the right rein far out to her right. As she began another smooth turn I pulled against her shoulder with the spur and kept her head held to the right with the single rein. She spun almost in her tracks and I brought the reins together above her mane and eased them back behind the saddle horn. She stopped. I looked at Richard who sat on the red roan who stood in the center of the round pen.

Richard nodded and said. "She's ready."

I eased the black filly into the center of the round pen. Using pressure with his legs Richard pushed the red roan into a lope and imitated the routine I had just completed with the black filly. He rode the red roan to the tall heavy gate, reached down with his left hand and released the latch which held it shut. The black filly and I followed Richard and the red roan to the dirt road and north to the river. The small black coarse haired dog that Richard called Jeepers trotted behind the black filly.

"'want to count the cattle and winter calves." Richard said as opened the wire gate, led the red roan through and held the gate while I followed on the black filly. Richard leaned his right shoulder against the Bois d'arc post to which the barbed wire which made up the gate was attached. The wire strained against the post and his shoulder. But Richard reached around the Bois d' arc post, gripped the back of the heavy crosstie which formed the stretch post of the fence and forced the wire loop over the top of the Bois d' arc post and fastened the gate. He stepped back up on the red roan. "May take some time because I want to see every cow and every calf." He looked at me.

"All-right. Every cow and every calf." I acknowledged.

Richard pushed the red roan into an easy lope. The black filly followed the red roan and we rode passed the windmill and the corrals, turned north and passed the battered old railcar which formed the western end of the upper corral and soon we descended the long sandy slope down into the Middle Field which twisted west along its narrow track following the southern outline of the range of sand hills which blocked the river from intruding upon it. We exited the western end of the Middle Field into the first shelter belt and Richard slowed the red roan to a steady walk as we moved between the two rows of Bois d' arc trees which the Works Progress Administration workers had planted during the Dust Bowl of the 1930's.

I touched the black filly with my spurs and she stepped up beside the red roan. "No sign of them yet." I stated the obvious to Richard.

"We'll check the far shelter belt and the west line." Richard said. He moved the red roan into a brisk walk and the lead again.

I followed them across the dry wet season creek and up the sandy trail which climbed to the far shelter belt. To my right I noticed movement. I shortened the black's reins and steadied myself in the saddle. A dozen wild turkeys trotted north away from us. The black ignored them and followed obediently after the red roan. Jeepers made a feint as if to pursue the turkey but he did not.

Richard smiled back at me. "'good idea to keep a short rein on her." He said. "Until you know what she'll do when somethin' busts from the brush."

Richard topped the rise and looked to his right into the beginning of the twin rows of Bois d' arc trees which formed this shelter belt too. I crossed the top and followed his gaze into this shelter belt.

Two yearling whitetail does dashed out the other side of the shelter belt with the white white of the underside of their tails flashing in the muted early winter sunlight and a porcupine, his flattened quills appearing black against his back, gazed down unalarmed at us from its perch two thirds up one of the Bois d' arc trees, but no cattle greeted us.

The red roan stepped out quickly, moving west. The black filly followed and Jeepers continued to run rear guard. The dog kept his head down and stepped each step in one of the horses' fresh prints. Thus he avoided most of the sharp grass burrs which plagued this side of the creek. The long double line of trees blocked the new north wind and the day still felt warm and soft until we passed the western end of the trees.

A cold steady north breeze pushed against our faces and my eyes watered. Richard frowned.

"They might be just west of us inside the salt cedars and out of the wind." I offered.

Richard looked at me and shook his head. He reined the red roan back to the shelter belt. This time we rested between the two lines of trees. Richard pointed at the ground and said. "No fresh sign. This time of year they would have gathered here before they went out on the river. They'd be some fresh sign." Richard looked over his left shoulder and stared at the dry river bed. "'wasn't enough sign along the creek to think they went out that way either." He spoke his thoughts out loud. "They're east. 'most probably along the sloughs south of the salt cedars, like you say." He sighed and continued to stare at the river. "'best way back there is along the edge of the river."

"I haven't heard any rifle shots. It's midday." I encouraged.

Deer season posited a very real danger to riders along the edge of the river. The river bed itself and the islands formed by the river's shifting narrow flows had been judged public hunting lands that could be accessed by motorized means. It was one of only two such rivers in Texas because geographers had determined that its headwaters were at the beginning of Tule Creek in eastern New Mexico. Thus, through some bizarre interpretation of federal preemption the Texas ban against motorized travel along or on a river bed could not be enforced and hunters scoured the river bed for miles east of the highway bridge where they unloaded their four wheelers and raced east eager to shoot anything which might ease out of the heavy salt cedars along the southern cut-bank, or, too often, anything large and moving along that southern cut-bank. Richard and I had made it a rule not to ride the river's edge during deer season, especially alone. Even cell phones gave no security that help could be summoned because they did not function below the cedars.

Now Richard stared at Doe Island which lay in the middle of the river and east of us. He reached back and began to untie his oilskin slicker from behind his saddle. I untied mine from behind my saddle. But I waited until he had snapped fastened the front flap of his and handed him my reins before I struggled into mine.

Richard chuckled. "She's doin' good."

I nodded in agreement. "And I don't want to do anything to give her cause not to."

Richard chuckled again and handed my reins back to me. He dug in the deep front wells of his slicker and extracted two scarves. Once smooth, sleek and silk squares of regal red and effervescent blue, the tattered and ripped red scarf had faded to a rusted orange and the torn thin blue scarf had faded to a melancholy azure by long exposure to the sun and wind and cold. He held the red scarf out to me. "Tie it on the outside. 'somewhere it can be seen." He instructed.

I took the scarf and draped it over the Charley Crazy Horse cavalry hat I wore and tied it underneath my chin while Richard tied the blue scarf around his left bicep.

Richard looked at me, shook his head and said. "If they shoot you there is one thing we will know for certain."

"What's that?"

"It wasn't an accident." He said and he turned the red roan north to the river. "Let's go."

Richard eased the red roan through the thick twist-tied salt cedars. The black filly snorted her dislike of the cedars, their closeness and their resistance, but she pushed through them behind the red roan. Jeepers walked along behind the black undisturbed by the matted limbs above him and grateful for the soft cushion of the thick salt grass beneath his feet. The north wind hit us hard for the first time as the horses emerged from the cedars and stood upon the narrow trail between the cedars and the cut-bank of the river's weak stream.

Richard surveyed the empty river bed. Nothing moved upon it. He reined the red roan east and held him to a steady walk. Despite the cold wind which slapped his face across his left shoulder he watched the river.

The trail narrowed, crossed the muddy mouth of the creek where it emptied into the river and clung ever closer to the edge of the cut-bank as the horses trudged eastward.

The salt cedars grew thicker, taller and impassable as we approached the eastern line of the pasture and the southern end of the destroyed old wooden bridge which had once crossed the river here. Only a few of the massive pylons which had once supported the timbers which formed the roadway of the bridge still protruded above the gathering sand of the slough.

Cattle, our cattle, lounged against the low sand berm which had formed around the pylons. Others grazed in the shallow swell which ended against the berm. Others moved about in the slough grass beyond the end of the salt cedars.

Richard held the red roan on short rein. "We need to be east of them." Richard said. He studied the river bed just beyond the pylons which formed the northern edge of the slough. A stagnant pool of salty water stood against their northern bases. "'can't tell how solid it is." He said.

"No. You can't." I agreed. 'And you can't ride a horse out on it until you know.' I thought. The captain had pounded it into us until we held at as a sacred pledge to him.

'Never. Never. Ride a horse onto the Big Red. Lead him. If you walk into quicksand you can flop onto your belly and float out. A horse can't!'

Not ten years ago Charley Haze and two young cowboys had tried to ride across the Big Red from the north not a mile west. Two horses had stepped into quicksand. Charley had held to his horse's reins and managed to turn the horse around and whip the poor creature until he finally floundered out of the quicksand, winded and so weak Charley had to lead him. The other horse was not blessed with an experienced rider. The boy had leaped from his saddle and struggled back to the edge of the quicksand. The horse had panicked. The big strong bay had pitched ten more yards into the wide stream of the quicksand before his strength was exhausted.

Charley had tried to save the bay. Charley had stripped naked, held the loop of one of the two lariats he had tied together to have enough rope to reach the bay horse in his left hand and wallowed on his belly out to the horse. Charley had snugged the loop to the trapped horse's saddle horn. Charley had rolled to the front of the horse like some great red breaded wiener, grasped the horse's reins and struggled desperately to coax, pull and jerk the bay's head around while the third horse and the bay's rider had pulled with all their strength against the rope.

But the bay had lost any faith in any of them. He refused to be turned. He pitched forward time and time and further and further into the quicksand, until his great head had fallen forward into the water which he had flailed free of the quicksand and which floated atop it now. Blood trickled from both of the horse's nostrils.

Charley had wormed his way back to the two boys. He reached into his pants pocket. "Son." He said to the wide eyed boy. "Take your clothes off. Go get your saddle."

"But my horse?"

Charley Haze had shaken his head. "Your horse is lost, son. I am sorry." Charley opened the large blade of his pocket knife and locked it in place. "His lungs are gone. There's blood coming from his nose. We can leave him to die. Or…" Charley hesitated. "We can help him." Charley trembled. "Now go get your saddle. I'll do the rest." He commanded.

The boy had wept as he had crawled out to his horse and found the latigo by feel and freed it from the brass loop. He had wept louder as he had drug it behind him as Charley Haze crawled passed him to slit his horse's throat.

Leading his horse with the other horse carrying both boys Charley had reached the old house where the half barn now stood three hours later. The captain was there and Richard.

The captain had grabbed come-alongs, ropes and ordered Richard to saddle Button, the young strong thoroughbred bay, and made haste for the river. They had found the boy's bay, lying on his side in the slough grass a hundred yards from the quicksand. He had bled to death from the knife wound in his neck. When they backtracked to the quicksand it was apparent the bay had pitched his way across the quicksand after Charley and the two boys had abandoned him. The horse's will to live had been great and it had freed him from nature's quicksand, but it could not free him from human ignorance.

Richard said that the captain had cursed Charley Haze and, though the captain was almost seventy-five by then, had threatened to tie Charley to a salt cedar and whip him with a reata, and the boy had knelt by his horse, looked up at the captain and asked, "What do we do now?" And the captain, being the captain, had said. "Not a goddamn thing. The coyotes and turkey buzzards will tend to him now." The captain had shaken his head and finished by saying. "Damn shame. Damn fine horse. 'be more justice in it if I left the three of you in that quicksand." Richard said he never saw that boy on a horse again and Charley Haze had not spoken to the captain again, though he did attend the captain's funeral.

"I'll ease south along the cedars and try to get around 'em on that end." Richard said. He nodded at the loose sandy berm in front of the pylons. "See if she can soft foot across that berm and get you east of 'em on this end." He moved the red roan back into the edge of the salt cedars and walked him south.

I touched the black filly with my spurs. She stepped to the edge of the sandy slope leading to the top of the wind made dune and started to climb. The sand slipped beneath her hooves. Instead of stopping the filly lunged up the slope. The cattle stirred, then spooked as the black filly flung sand behind her as she drove herself to the top of the sand dune.

"Shit!" I cursed. "'got to get east of them." I urged the filly on across the top of the berm. She surged forward and we passed east of all the cattle but one.

The half-Longhorn heifer flew east and disappeared into the scrub cedars, beetle brush and tall Indian and switch grass which outlined the cedars and the brush in the slough.

I pushed the last cow and her newborn calf passed Richard and the red roan and onto the trail the cattle used to return to the windmill and fresh water. Richard noted his count on the palm of his left hand.

"That's all of them but that one half Longhorn heifer that broke east when we jumped them." I said.

The cattle strung out behind the old horned Hereford cow, the acknowledged herd leader. The horned Hereford cow struggled up the steep sandy slope of the northernmost sand hill. She followed the deep trail which many hooves had cut by using it to return from the slough whose native tall blue stem grass greened first in the spring to the windmill's fresh water. The herd obediently followed her.

Richard stacked his hands on his saddle's horn and looked over his shoulder east back along the slough. "Did she have a calf with her?" He asked.

"I don't know." I answered. "She was going so damn hard through the brush I couldn't tell if anything was following her."

"Do you think she had a bag?"

"As best I could tell."

Richard sighed. "We need to know."

I looked north across the cold dry salt river. "That norther's coming." A black wall stretched from the western horizon to the eastern horizon above the rock cliffs which formed the northern boundary of the Prairie Dog Town Fork of the Red River at this place. Following the slow advance of that black wall was gale force wind tipped with sharp sleet and cold cold cold, the kind of cold that kills.

Richard turned the red roan away from the trail to the windmill and home. He faced the slough.

"That storm will cut us off before we can get back." I warned him again. "And it's just one part Longhorn heifer. And if she's down trying to calve there won't be much we can do for her."

"If he lose but one of them, does he not leave the ninety and the nine in the wilderness, and go after the one which is lost, until he find it?" Richard touched the red roan with his spurs and trotted back across the berm and into the slough.

I laid my hand upon the black's mane. She followed the red roan. The black drew up alongside of the red roan.

"Thinking like that I'm not certain that the Lord would have made much money running cattle along the Prairie Dog Town Fork of the Red."

Richard smiled. "'maybe not. But he would have tended to each animal in his care."

We rode towards White's Creek to find the half Longhorn heifer. The storm's western edged moved ahead of the rest of the storm and hid the fading sun and pushed a cold and growing colder wind against our backs.

I glanced over my shoulder. On our way back the storm would strike us from the north northeast, coming across the dry river bed unimpeded and slashing into our weary horses' faces and Richard's and mine. I pushed the black and she quickened her pace.

"'can't outrun that storm and getting that horse too hot too quick will force you to ride slower going back into it." Richard warned.

I slowed the black. Richard was right. He usually was right.

As we approached White's Creek the berm began to grow and rise and block not only the flow of the river but sight of it as well. Richard had spotted fresh sign of the heifer, wet manure and sharp tracks. Now he saw alarming signs staining the manure and tracks, drops of blood which stained sweet smelling strings which lay atop the manure and the tracks. The heifer was close, close to use and close to calving.

I thought Richard would slow the red roan to ensure we did not ride across the heifer as she was delivering the calf. A first calf heifer with a newly calved calf can be unpredictable and aggressive. Instead Richard shoved his spurs against the red roan's ribs just in front of the horse's flanks and held them there. The roan moved into a quick lope.

I looked down and found the reason for that lope. Two dozen straight little round holes and a larger hoofed hole dotted the heifer's trail. A farrow sow with piglets was trailing the blood and strings being left by the heifer. And then the worst sign, big, deep, broad and disturbing, a boar was closing on the sow, her piglets, the heifer and, hopefully by now, her new born calf, because if these marauders came upon the heifer in the throws of delivering the calf, mother and child were in real danger of joining the heifer's afterbirth as the main course in a tearing, snorting, fierce meal.

Richard crossed over the high berm and disappeared down to the deep deer pool formed by White's Creek as it emptied into the river. The quiet across the berm from me exploded with what sounded as if a woman was screaming. These screams deepened into bellows which were joined by snorts, those of the red roan and deeper, more guttural snorts, and by squeals. All this was followed by Richard's cursing.

The red roan surged back across the berm, rider less. Jeepers dashed up the berm and disappeared down the other side into the den of noise. I reined the black at the berm and stuck her hard with my spurs. She charged up the berm. From its crest before me and across the deer pool I saw the wilding tumult.

Richard stood waist deep in the water on the far side of the deep deer pool, clutching the front legs of a newly born calf and struggling to keep its head above the water. On the steep bank just above Richard the heifer stood, head lowered, horns swinging from side to side, trying to warn away the sow who snorted and tried to sidle passed the heifer and to the bloody afterbirth which clung to the sage brush at the edge of the pool. The piglets squealed and swarmed around their mother.

I put the black into a steep slide down into White's Creek just above the deer pool. I eased passed the heifer. She remained focused upon the sow. I could see the boar in the brush a few yards beyond the heifer and the sow. I freed my rope from where it was tied to Boss's saddle just in front of my left leg and draped it around my neck and beneath my left shoulder. I stepped down from the black. I held her reins.

Richard was slipping further down into the deep deer pool. Soon the water would be too deep for him to keep the calf's head above the water. I knew Richard would make an attempt to save the calf, to lift it and carry it up the steep slick bank, whatever the odds were against that attempt succeeding and despite the risk it posed to him.

The uproar behind the black was growing in intensity and volume. Jeepers now added his high pitched cry to the bellows, squeals and snorts.

I rubbed the filly's neck. Her muscles danced with the tension of a supercharged high voltage cable; ground it, set that electricity free in those taut strong young muscles and she would be gone. Nothing, no barbed wire wrapped cut bit, no head downing slamming of the left rein to the rider's hip, nothing could then hold her here amidst the wild confusion which was beginning to flail about only steps behind her back hocks. Only her own will to stand and stay held her in place now.

I blew my breath into my cheeks, let it whistle passed my lips, draped the reins around the filly's neck, unraveled several rounds of the rope, double wrapped the knotted end of the rope around the saddle horn, worked the knot through this wrap and pulled the knot hard against the wrap. Tied fast and true, there was no chance it would slip nor hope it would release if the black horse broke and ran. I worked the loop on the other end of the rope down across my shoulder, freed my arm and snugged the loop against my chest.

Using the rope as a guide wire hand over hand I backed down the slope and stepped behind Richard. He, too, trembled, but not from fright but from wet cold exhaustion.

Chaos reigned behind the black. Jeepers had made the black his Alamo. He had drawn an invisible line in the dirt some six inches behind the filly's back legs. Each time the enraged sow approached this line the little dog flashed into her, his high pitched voice screaming with his own fury and his teeth snapping and slashing; he would force the sow to retreat.

The exhausted heifer used these temporary engagements by the dog to suck for breath through her wide flared frothed nostrils which hung only a few inches above the torn ground. As soon as the small black dog dashed back into the tall blue stem grass to safety the embattled heifer charged back into the churning mass of sow, piglets and now the blood lusting boar.

The half Longhorn would drop one side or the other of her sharp pointed horns and lung at anything within range. Most often she missed and drove the side of her head hard into the ground. Sometimes she staggered and sank to her front knees, but from somewhere beyond natural sources she would summon strength enough to rise again and stagger back to the edge of the deep pool, believing her newborn calf safe there, unaware that if Richard weakened her calf would drown.

The boar charged. Jeepers answered with his charge. But this time the little dog was too slow. The boar's tusk snagged the dog just behind the dog's left shoulder, lifted the dog off of the ground and flung him screeching with pain into White's Creek.

"Damn!" Richard cursed. "'boar got the Jeepers."

I looked down and watched black blood tangled pieces of hair float passed Richard's boots.

The boar's victory was momentary. The heifer seized the moment, aimed the tip of one long lance of horn at the boar's midsection and charged. She struck the boar in his right flank, pierced the loose flesh and tried to lift the impaled wild hog into the air. The trembling heifer was too weak to lift the heavy boar. She staggered onto her front knees again. But as she collapsed the determined mother drove her spear through the other flank of the thrashing boar and trapped his hind quarters beneath her blood splattered head.

The boar roared. He tore himself free of the horn, ripping both of his flanks open. They spewed blue black blood across the face and horns of the heifer. Wild with pain the boar turned now upon his children. He seized the closest piglet and crushed it between his jaws. He chewed upon the writhing piglet, tore its midsection free and swallowed his child's intestines as the piglet died beneath him.

The sow seeing that the boar now posed the threat to her young surged into the boar and drove him onto his side. She clamped her jaws upon the boar's ear. He slashed her face and shoulders with his razor sharp tusks. Because of this she withdrew. But she did not release his ear. She tore the ear from the boar's head. He railed with pain and fury. Now blood spouted from the side of his head as well as each of his flanks.

I worked the rope underneath the calf and against Richard's left side.

"That black breaks and..." Richard's voice surrendered to a shivering chatter.

"I know." I wrapped my right arm around Richard's skinny waist and gripped the rope. "Let's see if we can climb up using the rope."

Richard nodded.

"Right foot first."

We raised our right feet, pushed them up the slope six inches and thrust our weight onto them as struggled to lift our left feet free of the sucking mud. Our weight, the calf's unwieldy weight, the slope, its angle and its slickness, caused our right boots to slide back. Only the deep sets left from where we had lifted our boots moments before stopped our slide. Our boots settled back into the sets.

"'not working." Richard's teeth chattered.

I looked at the filly. Behind her the heifer still knelt on her front knees. Her sides heaved from her desperate breathing. The wounded boar decided to gorge himself on another of his offspring and the sow moved at him again in an attempt to save yet another of her dead children.

"It's fixin' to go to hell up there." Richard coughed.

I pressed my lips and sucked noisily through them. The filly's alert ears came forward and her dark eyes shone with a wild light as she lowered her head and stared down at me. I made the sound again and commanded. "Back black. Back."

The filly jerked her head up and I could see the muscles along her neck ripple beneath her glossy black coat.

"No horse! Not even old Aztec! Would back into that!" Richard hissed through his teeth which he had clenched to stop them from chattering.

"She ain't no horse." I said. "She's the black." I sucked through my lips and asked again. "Back."

She backed.

Each step was a step into the unknown for the black because she kept her gaze fixed on Richard, the heifer's calf and me until she had pulled us free of the deep deer pool. Then she looked over her shoulder and snorted at the hogs fighting behind her.

I pushed Richard against the black's side and she returned her attention to us. Richard lifted the newborn calf and draped it across the saddle. He tried to place his left boot into the stirrup. But my stirrups were too short for him to reach it. I cupped my hands together and braced them against my knees. Richard placed his boot in my hands and I lifted and he swung his right leg across the saddle until he was seated behind the calf. I grabbed the black's reins and skirted the killing field being created by the boar upon his children and waded across the shallow end of the deep deer pool. The black followed.

With White's Creek and the deep deer pool providing some safety between us the half-Longhorn heifer, the boar, the sow and what remained of her piglets I stopped the black and looked up at Richard.

Richard slumped forward against the calf with his hands resting on my saddle's wide horn. He looked down at me and said. "'see if you can pick up the roan's track. Maybe he didn't go too far and at least he was traveling the right direction."

"Jeepers?" I asked.

Richard swallowed and shook his head. "'doubt he made it. And we can't afford to look for him." Richard nodded to the west. A wall of black clouds confronted our gazes. "We're soaked and pretty much spent. 'less time we give that norther to blast away at us the better we will be for it."

I nodded, glanced over my shoulder but caught not a glimpse of the small black dog. The heifer was still focused on the battling hogs. "How do we get the heifer to follow?" I asked.

"'start walkin'. I'll get her to come." Richard said.

I stepped in front of the black and started back along the trail we had ridden earlier. The baby calf cried out. I looked back. Richard twisted its wet tail again and again the baby cried. The heifer answered the call, tentatively, softly at first, then louder and with recognition. The heifer turned and began to wade across White's Creek.

"Get goin'!" Richard commanded.

I stepped forward and began to walk. The black raised her head, jerked against her reins and whinnied. I gripped the reins to jerk her head down, but before I could I heard the answering whinny and the red roan trotted forward to greet the black. He lowered his head, submitting to the filly. She rubbed the bottom of her jaw along the top of his neck.

Richard laughed. "Well. 'hope he knows from now on she'll be the boss of him." Richard swung down from the black. He left the calf draped across my saddle. "Step up." He said. "Before mama gets here and we end up in another fight."

The heifer was now standing on our side of White's Creek and calling to her calf. I gripped the tie strings on the left of my saddle, leaned back, stabbed my left foot into the stirrup and hauled myself up into my saddle. Richard tossed his unbroken right rein around the red roan's neck, gripped the half length remaining of his left rein, stuck his foot into the tapedero covered stirrup of his saddle and stepped up and swung into his saddle.

"Ride ahead." Richard said. "I'll ride rear guard against the heifer."

I smooched to the black and she stepped forward. The calf called again to the mother it had yet to see and the heifer called back and started to us. Richard put the red roan between her and the black and our caravan began its retreat from White's Creek.

A quarter of a mile from the deep deer pool the angry norther snatched the black's reprieve from us. Half of the wind driven drops splashed against our faces and soaked what little of our clothing which had not been soaked by the deer pool's water. The other half cut into our faces with their frozen edges. It was the worst of its kind, half frozen rain being hurled into us before the hard frozen sleet within the body of the storm reached us.

The black hesitated when the norther slapped her in the face.

"'keep her movin'." Richard urged.

I pushed the rawls of my spurs against the black's ribs. But she refused. I lifted my legs away and prepared to stick the steel harder into her tender ribs.

Richard called. "Look to your left! The heifer sees something."

'Christ! What could this be?' I thought. But I looked left.

Jeepers hobbled forward from the brush. He sat down beside the red roan and looked up at Richard. Blood soaked his back and right side. I could see flesh beneath the thick coarse black hair along his shoulder.

Richard slapped his leg and Jeepers struggled up and raised himself up onto his back legs with his left front paw balanced against Richard's stirrup. Richard reached down, seized him by the scruff of his neck and lifted him onto the saddle in front of him. Jeepers spread his body across the saddle, whined and rested his chin on Richard's chaps.

"How bad is he torn up?" I asked.

"Bad enough." Richard replied. "But he's a tough old fart. I think he'll make it."

I shoved my spurs into the black. She snorted, shook her head with displeasure, but stepped forward and led our march into storm and for home. We hoped.

"We're at the old bridge." I shouted over my shoulder to Richard. But he could not hear me above the wail of the wind coming from the river. I backed the black alongside the red roan, leaned to Richard and shouted again. "The old bridge!" I pointed at the ghostly pylons which were almost veiled by the sleet and rain.

Richard nodded and glanced over his shoulder and a dozen yards behind us the heifer stood with her head down.

"Can she climb the trail up the sand hill?" I asked.

The heifer did not appear as if she could walk the fifty yards to the trail, much less climb the one hundred feet up the steep trail with the loose giving blow sand sliding away from her hooves with each step.

"She'll climb for him." Richard said. He reached across and stroked the baby calf draped over the front of my saddle. "She's a good mother."

We sat at the bottom of the steep sand hill which separated the slough and the pasture.

"Let me make the top. Then you come up." Richard said. He shoved his hands against the red roan's neck and the horse started up the sand hill.

I watched the red roan climb. Half-way up the horse began to surge, throwing his front legs forward and gathering his back legs underneath him in a quick strong thrust. Horse and rider disappeared over the crest of the hill, then returned and stood to the side of the trail to allow the black and I room to pass.

I reined the black to the trail. She looked up at Richard and the red roan. She sighed, took one step up the trail and without hesitation began to surge upward. I grabbed the saddle horn with my left hand, balanced the calf with my right, leaned forward and struggled to stay balanced on the saddle as the black flung herself and her cargo up the trail. The black shot across the crest of the hill, too, like the red roan unable to stop short of it. I reined her about and eased her beside Richard and the red roan.

The half-Longhorn heifer stood at the bottom of the trail. She looked to her left and to her right, and stepped to her right as if to abandon her pursuit and return to the slough.

"Rouse that baby. 'get a bawl out of him." Richard ordered.

I shook the baby calf until he bawled, once, twice. Before his third cry the heifer was climbing the trail.

"She's comin'." Richard said. "Let's go."

We turned the horses and began the long wet cold walk to the windmill and the old corrals to the south.

The norther continued to batter sleet and ice against our backs. The horses trudged passed the windmill, stopped out the watering trough and lowered their heads to the icy water. The hot exhaust of their heavy breathing thawed the flimsy ice which was forming on the top of the water and the horses drank deep and slow.

The heifer appeared from the dark storm. "Ride into the upper lot. Lay her baby at the edge of the old feeding bunks. I'll hold her back 'till you get remounted and back out the gate." Richard lifted the red roan's nose from the water and turned to face the heifer.

I urged the black away from the water. She trotted into the upper lot. I stepped down hard from the saddle and slid the calf off the saddle and into my arms. As I laid him against the old disheveled feed bunk he bawled.

"Hurry up!" Richard called. "I can't hold her away for long."

I struggled back up into the saddle, turned the black and rode for the gate. Before I could pass through the gate the heifer stormed through, followed by Richard's warning. "Look out! Let her through!" I reined the black to the side and passed beside the heifer as she trotted through the gate, calling to her calf. The calf returned her call. I glanced over my shoulder and saw the heifer nuzzling her child.

Richard rode the red roan through the gate which I held open against the gusting north wind and blowing rain. I fastened the gate, remounted and turned the black south on the dirt road. The red roan stepped in behind the black. Aligned, the tired horses began the last leg of the journey.

With night, wind, rain and fatigue weighing all down, the horses trudged forward with their heads held low. I glanced over my shoulder.

Richard's shoulders were hunched forward and drawn into his chest, his hands lay piled upon the saddle's horn with his arms resting across Jeepers' bloody back, his head was drooped forward and his hat hid his face. I wondered if he was asleep and whether he was secure on his saddle. But I turned back, allowed my head to tilt forward and my shoulders too to sag. The wind cried behind us. The half-frozen rain pelted down upon us. And the cold crept through us. The horses struggled on.

A hundred yards or so before we reached the gate which led to the corrals and the barn the horses either whiffed the sweet smell of the remains of that mornings leavings in their stalls or they sensed the proximity of the barn, feed and rest. The black's head came up and she stepped into a quick walk. The red roan abandoned the luxury of trailing immediately behind the black and moved up beside her. Any other time and Richard would have rebuked the red roan for even hinting at becoming barn sour. But he made no move to reprimand the horse and I allowed the black to continue to quicken her pace until we trotted through the gate and to the east end of the barn.

I slid down from the black and ground hitched her. I walked to the red roan. Richard was asleep. I shook him awake, slid Jeepers from beneath Richard's arms and set the dog upon the ground as Richard straightened his shoulders. "We made the barn." I told him. He nodded and dragged his leg across the roan roan's rump and dismounted.

He dropped the red roan's broken reins on the ground and limped toward the bathroom underneath the barn. "Strip off." I called after him. "I'll start a fire in the tire ring, then take care of the horses." He nodded and kept limping to the bathroom. He was soaked through, bitterly tired and his broken leg ached him. I knew he was exhausted because it was the only time I ever saw him walk away from a hot horse without first having unsaddled him and cared for his needs.

I had unsaddled the red roan, brushed him dry, placed him in his stall and forked a heavy flaking of alfalfa into his stall when Richard emerged from the bathroom. He had a heavy tattered stained robe wrapped around him and he was wearing slippers not his boots and no hat. His long gray hair was still damp and it roped down along his cheeks and across the back of his crinkled neck. He eased down into one of the canvas chairs which I had stationed beside the rear tractor tire ring in which I had built a mesquite wood fire. Jeepers crept to the fire and lay beneath Richard's chair.

As I returned to the black I stuck my left boot into the stirrup. I noticed she turned her head and eyed me as I pulled myself back up onto the saddle. I eased her up to the fire ring and Richard. I folded my hands on the saddle horn, looked down at Richard and sighed. "Richard…" Left! I sensed it more than I felt it. Left, right, a whirl and I lay on my back on the ground beneath the barn.

I rolled onto my side and pushed myself up to sit on my butt in the dust and alfalfa chafe and the dried remnants which Richard or I had spilled from the wheelbarrow's muck. "Agh! She did it to me again!" I rubbed my lower back and glared at the black who stood quietly chewing a loose flake of the alfalfa she had found on the barn's floor. "You threw me! Again! You damn horse!"

The black flicked her ears, stared at me and continued to chew.

I sat on the dirt of the barn's floor and angrily asked. "Well. What do I do now?"

Richard warmed his hands on the heat rising from the fire blazing within the tractor tire ring, shifted the dip against the inside of his lip and said. "'name her."

"What?"

"Name her."

"Why?" I asked.

"'cause if you keep callin' her 'damn horse' she's going to think that's her name." Richard spat into the fire. "And it seems you are going to keep calling her that 'cause it seems you are destined to keep falling off your horse." He looked at me and said. "So name her."

"Name her?"

Richard nodded.

"I cannot imagine what I would call her other than 'damn horse'."

Richard chuckled. "That won't do." He said. He warmed his hands, thought for several minutes and said. "Grace. 'call her Grace."

"Grace! Why in the world would I call this damn horse Grace?"

Richard massaged the dip against his inner lip and said. "'cause only by her grace are you and I here." Richard looked at me and smiled. "And only by her grace are you going to be able to stop falling off of her."

5.

I stood beside Richard on the platform above the round pen. We watched his daughter ease the raw Palomino colt around and around and around the pen.

I put my hand on Richard's shoulder. "Well. We may not have been much as husbands, but we certainly helped make some beautiful daughters."

"That's for sure." Richard agreed without taking his eyes away from his daughter and the young horse she rode. "Soft hands. Soft. Keep them soft and low." He murmured too softly for her to hear.

But as if she did hear her father's instructions, the girl lowered each hand until they floated just above the horse's neck.

"She rides like you." I said.

Richard nodded. He continued to watch the horse and the rider.

"Maybe better than you." I said as the girl sat quiet and still in the saddle even though the nervous colt surged and charged around the pen.

Richard turned to me and his smile was bright and full, filled with great satisfaction that this rare gift, his gift, his child had so completely assimilated.

I smiled, too. But my smile saddened as I realized that I had no such gift to give my child.

6.

"Look at this damn thing." I held the Agricultural Census Report I had been attempting to complete for an hour.

Richard grunted. "Why don't you just throw it in the trash barrel and burn it?"

"I did. Twice. Now they say if I don't complete it and mail it in you go to prison." I pointed at the red warning stenciled onto the front of the government form. "FAILURE TO REPORT CAN RESULT IN CRIMINAL SANCTIONS."

"Not me! You!" Richard retorted. "They mailed it to you."

"You forget. I'm an attorney. I'll cut a deal and give you up."

Richard laughed. "What's the next question?"

"Did you raise any ducks, geese, chickens, guineas, pea fowl or other poultry?" I looked at Richard. "'got any ducks, geese, other assorted poultry hidden under that piece of shit travel trailer?" I pointed at the battered travel trailer parked in the northwest corner of the barn which Richard lived in.

"Nope. Just a pair of quail, a rooster and a little hen. They come in the barn each morning."

"Don't feed 'em." I said. "They'll have us counting them, too!" I turned the page and stared at the words on the printed form. "In God's name!" I cried.

"What's wrong now?" Richard asked.

"My God! They want to know if we used any animal waste as fertilizer. And, if so, what type and how much." I looked at Richard and shook my head. "The damn government wants to know how much shit we spread!"

"How are you going to answer that?"

"Like this." I said. I wrote on the form. "Yes. The amount is equal to the capacity of twelve horses to defecate twice a day multiplied by three hundred and sixty-five days, adjusted by an occasional day or two when one or more horses colic and can't shit."

"You really gonna' send that in?" Richard laughed.

"Hell yes." I replied. I closed the form, folded it, stuffed it into the wrong size pre-addressed envelope provided and sealed the envelope. "Richard. We live in the most socialistic state ever concocted."

Richard nodded. "We ask for it every time we take a hand out from the government."

I sighed. I walked to the pick-up, shoved the envelope on top of the papers cluttering the dash above the steering wheel and hoped I remembered to mail it.

7.

The snow had come during the night after the wind had slipped from a gale to a steady norther. Large serpentine flakes rich with nitrogen and heavy with moisture still danced down through the yellow haze of the yard light and settled upon the eight inches already accumulated on the gravel of the yard behind the half-barn and in front of the abandoned old house. Somewhere amidst that snow, standing on three legs, his injured left hind leg cradled beneath him, Mary Beth Wadley's fine bay horse, Whiskey, struggled to stay on his feet, his instinct telling him that to lie down in snow meant to die in snow.

The pilot of the Salt Creek Ranch helicopter had spotted the injured horse sulled in the sloughs just before sunset. But spot the horse was all he could do. Darkness and snow grounded the helicopter. To bring Whiskey out of the sloughs in a blizzard alive would require a horseman, a man who not only rode by instinct but knew horses by instinct as well. And Mary Beth knew only one such man. She called Richard.

The black stamped her feet, unaccustomed to the cold snow which surrounded her ankles.

"You don't have to come." Richard said as he tightened the cinch against Harley's belly. The big red roan nodded his head twice as though he was telling Richard. "Tight enough." Richard agreed and fastened the cinch.

"I know." I rubbed the black's belly until she exhaled. Then I tightened her cinch. I pulled the waterproofed ski gloves onto my hands, rubbed the black's face and led her towards the dirt road which led to the river and its sloughs.

Richard smiled and followed, leading Harley. Once on the road Richard and I mounted and rode north. Harley sought the lead, but the black refused his claim. Thus the two horses long trotted side by side.

"I thought you were leaving Jeepers behind." I pointed over my shoulder at the hairy black dog which raced after the horses.

"Damn you. If you give out I'll leave your ass on the river." Richard cursed the dog who now trotted immediately behind Harley. "Suit yourself." He said to the dog and turned back around in the saddle.

"He is. Besides, maybe he knows where Whiskey is." I teased Richard.

Jeepers matched his stride to the big red roan's stride and we marched north on the dark snowy sandy road to the river pasture.

Richard reached down, unsnapped the snap ring which held together the ends of the chain which fastened the gate to the river pasture, pushed the gate open, turned Harley so he could catch the gate with his right hand and refasten it behind us without dismounting, which he did. He clucked Harley back into a trot. The black resumed her trot beside the big horse, still determined not to be relegated to following his lead. Jeepers continued to trot behind the bay.

Through the darkness the horses followed the snow catching twin ruts of the pasture road until they reached the top of the first shelter belt where Richard turned Harley into the long dark line of trees.

"Watch your head." Richard warned as Harley twisted around the occasional wayward mesquite which had found root between the tandem lines of Bois d'arc and American elm trees which made up the shelter belt.

Twilight, dampened by the falling snow, hazed the outline of the trees. The north wind could not reach inside the shelter of the trees. The large snowflakes flittered, floated and twisted down in an uncertain and eerily quiet snowfall. The taller elm trees hid the snow which burdened there highest limbs and caused these limbs to cast enlarged early morning shadows across the prickly pear which broke up the thin white pallet of the floor of the shelter belt.

The black darted around the painful palms of the prickly pear and kept pace with the red roan and the dog as we hurried west to the end of the trees to cross the creek which bounded this shelter belt on its western most edge.

As we crossed the dry creek I looked over my shoulder. The rising sun streaked random rays horizontally beneath the canopy. The rays lighted the snow laden limbs of the Bois d'arc and mesquite trees. Yellowish light glowed as if from relumed dismembered ancient lamps.

The snow did not fill the ruts of the ranch road which separated the Hackberry, mesquite and Juniper tree thicket from the south side of the second shelter belt. The road, being on the lee side of the shelter belt, had caught only a dusting of snow. Trapped between the shelter belt and the copse of trees and canopied by the snow which blew across the tops of the taller trees of the shelter belt and slid down the northern trunks of the lesser mesquites and the heavy evergreen limbs of the junipers, the road captured a curious calmness. The horses' hooves called in cadence as if they were soldiers being marched on the double quick into some unseen battle.

The horses exited the natural pergola and Richard turned the red roan right. We descended into a deep gully with almost a foot of snow covering the trail which ran along its bottom and led us to the southern edge of the slough. Richard turned west along the narrow ledge between the barbed wire fence and the old high water cut where the charred remnants of an ancient volcanic explosion in eastern New Mexico, lost even to the time explorers of today and their radioactive prying, continued to block the eroding water from evaporating the sandy loam of the prairies. There, before farmers and government imposed terracing of their fields slowed and diverted its course, the water had rolled unimpeded off of the grass sod of the short grass prairies and had filled the normally dry river bed to flood.

The ledge narrowed until, and by some strenuous reining, I forced the black to yield the lead to the red roan and Jeepers. At the westernmost protrusion of the ancient volcanic rock Richard stopped. I allowed the black to ease up beside Richard and the red roan.

"'rest 'em here." Richard said, speaking of the horses. "Then we drop off and push through the salt cedars to the river." He nodded at the wall of white tinted grey salt cedars which blocked the way with there twisted trunks and intertwined lashes of corded branches. "We'll ride along the cut bank at the river's edge as far as we can. It'll be the easiest goin' for the horses there."

"And the coldest for us." I complained.

Richard ignored me. He slackened his reins to allow the red roan to stretch his black nostrils down to the snow which lay atop the tough salt grass which matted the top of the volcanic rocks upon which the horses stood. Jeepers yawned, lay down and curled up in the last tracks the red roan had made before he stopped. The little dog closed his eyes.

The black refused to let him sleep. She stretched her nose down to Jeepers and blew her hot breath into his face. Jeepers raised his head, frowned, turned over and, with his face away from the black's, closed his eyes again.

I lowered my chin onto my chest and dozed until I heard the red roan step off of the shelf of rock and I felt the black step forward across Jeepers to follow the red roan and I heard Jeepers growl his displeasure at the filly for stepping over him. I raised my chin, blinked, picked up my reins and stopped the filly until Jeepers trotted from beneath her and resumed his place at the heels of the red roan. I released the reins and the black filly stepped quickly off of the shelf and caught up to the red roan.

Richard pushed the heavy branches of the cedars aside, leaned forward and reined the red roan into the quiet darkness of the thick cedars. The black hesitated, intimidated by the solidity of the wall of trees before her. I lifted the reins, touched her with my spurs and smooched to her. She stepped into the inviolate realm of the slough's salt cedars.

The red roan twisted around clutching cedar trunks and beneath wet clinging threads of tough sinewy cedar limbs. I put the black in his track and encouraged her with soft touches of my spurs as she hesitantly followed the red roan and Jeepers through the salt cedars.

As we emerged on the river side of the cedars I could see the almost snow hidden cattle trail which

Richard had followed through the cedars. The river's single stream glistened against the cut bank fifty yards to our north. We were in the river's slough, amidst the winter's remains of horse belly high old blue stem and Indian switch grass, tramping across a carpet of dormant side oats and little Indian switch grasses which would bloom in early spring. A cold north wind blew into our faces.

I raised the right side of the collar of the heavy oilskin slicker to shield my face from the wind and snow as Richard again turned west. Now the filly was content with the big roan breaking the trail for her through the deepening snow. The wind gusted and increasing volleys of snow pelted against the right side of Richard's, mine and the horses' faces. The tall Indian switch grass shielded Jeepers' face as he stepped from track to track left by the red roan. The filly yielded, turned her face down and to the left, and trudged blindly behind the big roan horse which strode, head held high, through the heavy snow.

The black almost failed to see the red roan veer left into the wide shallow mouth of the wet weather creek. She made a quick left to stay in his track and I had to grab the saddle horn to stay centered. The black raised her head and I shortened her rein. We passed back through the salt cedars which were thinned and dispersed here by the occasional flow of the creek.

The creek narrowed and deepened as we approached the barbed wire fence. At the fence in the center of the creek the water gap had been almost subsumed by the silt brought there during last spring's storms. Some six feet above the silted gap, the bottom string of sharp barbed wire snow danced, still strung taut across the creek.

Richard stopped and studied the loose wire at the bottom of the creek and the tight wire above. He stepped down from the red roan and walked to the wire. He reached up and lifted against the bottom wire of the fence. "I'll hold the wire. You lead the horses through the gap one at a time." He instructed me.

I slid down from the black, grasped her left rein in my right hand and stepped across the mesh of wire on the bottom of the gap. The filly tiptoed across it, dropping her head only to duck under the bottom wire of the fence which Richard held aloft. I wrapped the black's rein in and out of a wild plum bush which clung to the side of the creek bed and walked back to lead the red roan across the gap.

The big horse approached the gap slowly, stopped and stared at the bottom strand of wire which seemed centered at his chest. I pulled the other rein off of his neck and grasped both reins in my right hand. Richard strained to raise the bottom strand of wire higher. I pulled against the reins. The horse stood. I looked at Richard.

"Put your arm around his neck and let him lower his head to your chest." Richard said.

I did so. Harley dropped his face to mine.

"Rub his neck."

I rubbed his neck.

"Now scratch him between his eyes."

I raised my hand to scratch between Harley's eyes. He lifted his head. I waited. He dropped it back. And I scratched between his eyes.

"Now try him. I think he will let you lead him through."

I eased the big horse across the gap as Richard lifted hard against the bottom wire to pass it just above the saddle horn.

Richard released the wire and stepped through the gap. I handed Harley's reins to him and asked. "What made him follow me?"

"Trust." Richard said. "'horse's eyes are set on the sides of his head. 'gives him great peripheral vision, but he can't focus on your hand when you scratch between his eyes. So you have to have his trust before he will let you do that. Once he let you scratch between his eyes and it felt good to him he trusted you and he followed you through the gap."

Richard and I remounted and rode south along the creek bed for a hundred yards or so until Richard swung the red roan up the shallow west wall of the creek. Richard sat on the red roan and watched the black step up out of the creek. We sat the horses and surveyed the snowy landscape.

East of the creek thick grey salt cedars crusted with snow penetrated south into the silted flood plain of the creek for a half mile and east away from us for a mile. This tangled trash land appeared to be and was mostly impenetrable.

"'hurt horse would be hard pressed to move into that. Unless he was hurt there and couldn't get out." Richard said and turned the red roan to face westward. "We'll start here." Richard pointed at the mattering of leafless wild plum thickets interspersed with occasional mesquites and some salt cedars which composed much of the terrain west of the creek. "Then swing south and back to the east." Richard stretched his back, "If need be."

I smiled, relieved not to be engaging the wall of salt cedars behind us immediately and hopeful we would find Whiskey to the west.

"See those three tall cottonwoods." Richard pointed at three tall sparsely limbed trees a mile or more northwest of us. "That's the far corner of this place and there's a fresh water seep there. That's why the cottonwood trees grow there. We go there first." Richard lifted the red roan's reins and the horse stepped forward. Jeepers followed the red roan and the black and I assumed our place at the rear. "Watch for sign." Richard called back to me.

"For tracks?" I asked.

"Unless they're real fresh tracks aren't as important as manure. 'pile of manure means he's rested there." Richard sighed. "For a while at least."

A seamless rug of snow covered the ground among the Buick size openings between the wild plum thickets, mesquite and cedar. Rabbit tracks poked tiny round holes into the deepening snow rug as it stacked higher into the center of the plum thickets. A coyote's circular paw print, faded by the fresh snowfall, tracked the rabbit's pin pricks into the plum thickets. But no horse's track, new or old, and no droppings, besides the scattered round pellets of several deer, appeared in the snow.

Richard rested the red roan underneath the cottonwood trees' skeletons and let him drink from the seep. Richard peered over his shoulder at the brutal barrier east of the creek. "'rest 'em here." He said. "If we have to go into those cedars." He nodded east. "They're gonna' need their strength to push through limbs and drifts."

I stared at the battlescape to our east. The snow flowed down upon the horses in layers of large wet flakes. The wind would rise from the stillness of the river to the north and whistle through the salt cedars and splash the snowy wafers of flakes against the sides of mine and Richard's faces as we stared to the east, and then die away to nothing. If we had to go east we would be tested, men, dog and horses.

We rode south. The horses moved in an almost straight line as the plum thickets and mesquites became separated by larger and larger open spaces. At the windmill and catch pens again we rested the horses and let them drink from the iron rimmed watering trough.

Richard stared at the top of the red roan's head as the horse drank from the trough.

"We haven't seen any sign of Whiskey."

"No. We haven't." Richard agreed. He continued to stare at the of Harley's head.

"What now?"

"Now." Richard said as he reined Harley away from the water trough. "Now." He repeated. "We go east."

I blew my breath out. "Snowing harder."

Richard nodded.

"Getting colder."

Richard nodded again. He pushed against Harley's neck and the big horse began to walk steadily east from the pens. He said nothing.

I turned the black and followed Richard, Harley and Jeepers. A half of a mile northeast we encountered the first of the salt cedars. A dozen steps farther and the horses began to twist and turn and push through the cedars whip like limbs. Farther into the cedars the footing became as if the horses were treading across the moors and the snow piled in deeper and deeper drifts in the smaller and smaller openings among the cedars which diminished to silver dollar size oasis of light amidst the dark seclusion of the snow bound salt cedar wilderness.

The black began to hesitate before she pushed through behind the red roan and the small black dog. As I urged the black through some tightly tangled salt cedar limbs I heard Richard call. "Here."

I pushed the black through the matted limbs and stopped her beside the red roan and Jeepers in the ten silver dollar size clearing. Whiskey's tracks faded into snow in half a dozen brush twisted trails in sight of where we sat. These trails divided into another two dozen serpentine trails and those trails divided into how many more.

I looked at Richard. "With this much snow in this heavy brush." I shrugged. I turned my face down as a cold cutting blast of snow passed. Staring at the black's shoulder I finished my thought. "It's just a guess which one leads to that horse." I looked at Richard again. "We've got three, maybe four hours of light left." I shrugged. "How many trails can we ride?"

"We'll split up. 'cover twice as many that way." Richard said.

"Then?"

Richard set his jaw, picked up his reins and said. "Then we ride in the dark." His eyes were clear and bright. "We ride until we do what we came to do. We ride until we find that horse." Cold, snow, wind, darkness; Richard would not stop or be stopped. He would find Whiskey.

Jeepers stood up, stretched and eased down one trail for a few yards, retreated, worked his way down the next, and repeated this routine several more times. Until on one trail he hesitated, sniffed at the drooping sage twice, and then trotted away down the trail.

Richard and I laughed. "Why not." Richard said.

We followed the dog as he trotted deeper and deeper into the thickening brush. The nettles, the thorns and the briars tore at our chaps as they slapped passed the horses' legs. A flash of bright color lost among the snow covered brush caught my eye. I leaned down and stared hard into the brush.

Richard reined Harley to a stop. "Hell. This is pointless. Who knows where he is going or why?" Richard grumbled. "Let's split up."

"Not yet. Not yet." I urged Richard as I rose up. "Jeepers is on a blood trail. It's oh so slight. 'almost can't be seen. But it's there and he knows it. Let's give him another ten minutes or so."

Richard nodded, picked up Harley's reins and continued to follow the little dog. Suddenly, Jeepers barked and raced ahead. Richard spurred Harley and Harley splashed through the snow as he charged after the dog. The black trotted behind.

Harley and the black burst from the brush into a small clearing and stopped. Jeepers sat in the middle of the clearing. He looked over his shoulder at the horses and Richard and I, and barked his high pitched bark twice and turned back to sniff at the large nose with which the big bay sniffed at his small hairy head.

Now Whiskey's life lay in a decision. Back-track through the slough. We could use the trail Harley had plowed. That would make the going easier. But with Whiskey injured as he was we would still have to go slow and night and cold would catch us before we could reach the barn, and with each step we would be moving father away from any help reaching us or Whiskey. If the pain and the fatigue became too much and Whiskey quit? I looked at the butt of the Winchester which protruded from Richard's saddle scabbard.

The alternative depended entirely upon Harley. Could the big horse continue to plow a way for us through the deepening snow to the road at the top of the Badley hill six miles away? The first four miles would twist around and through the stands of salt cedar which were causing deeper drifts on their lee sides which Harley would have to break through. The last two miles were a steep climb up from the river's slough to the road and rescue. This ride in good weather on dry turf with clear visibility would test many horses. But through now what had deepened to a foot or more of snow with drifts two to three feet deep and wet soggy ground beneath and trusting to Richard's navigational skills to pick the shortest, surest path, could the belligerent roan horse do this? He had already pushed his way through for many miles. Failure could mean leaving three horses to the snow's mercy. Was this asking too much of this good horse?

Richard slapped the snow from the bottom of his left boot, slipped that boot into the stirrup and stepped up into his saddle. He looked at our trail back to the slough. He touched Harley with his spurs and reined him away from the slough and into the unbroken snow. Bet it all to save Whiskey, bet it all on what Richard knew and understood---the strength and heart and will of the big roan horse.

For the first two miles Harley snow plowed through the loose snow whether it was a foot deep or wind stacked three feet deep and more. During the next mile Harley hesitated before each deep drift. Then he again plowed through these, also.

The black followed Harley, measuring her step so she did not walk up onto his heels. Whiskey walked behind the black with his head down, dragging his left hind leg through the snow. Jeepers brought up the rear.

Thus, we progressed three miles, snow covering the horses' manes and Richard and my shoulders and the white strands of hair which capped Jeepers' head, and the growing cold numbing our fingers and toes and hooves and paws. Until Harley stopped before a shallow drift, dropped his head, blew through his nose and did not plow into the drift when Richard lifted the reins.

Richard shook his right boot free of the snow encrusted tapedero and raised his butt off of the saddle.

"What are you doing?" I asked.

"'taking five." Richard answered.

"What the hell for!" I demanded. "You'll just get your boots wet."

"Because he's tired and I am going to let him rest." Richard snarled and swung down from the big horse.

I slid down from the black. Richard and I stood shoulder to shoulder and said nothing. Five minutes later he and I sat on our saddles with our shoulders with our backs humped against the wind blown snow which would have blinded us and maybe the horses had we still been pushing northeast through the salt cedars searching for Whiskey.

The windmill and pens seemed to rise up out of the snow this time as we approached them. Richard coaxed Whiskey to the watering trough and the tired, hurt horse trembled as he drank deeply. Richard stroked his neck.

"Do you think Harley can break us up and out to the road?" I asked and looked to the long steady climb south to the rural road which blocked our path to freedom and rescue.

Flashing through the blowing snow a black truck towing a long tandem trailer appeared, disappeared and reappeared. The diesel engine sagged as the truck and trailer engaged a snow drift, roared as it charged through the drift. The narrow rutted road down to the pens leaned at an increasing degree to the east before the road reached the flat floor of the river pasture. The black beast never hesitated, never faltered and never slowed to pick its way down this treacherous stretch of road. It raced, heedless of danger, to Richard and me and to our tired horses and the injured Whiskey.

"Hell of a way to break in a nice new rig like this." I greeted Kenneth Moorman as he climbed out of the shining cab of the big Dodge diesel truck.

"Little lawyer." Kenneth Moorman reached out and shook my hand. "I bought it to go where I want to go when I want to go there. If it's too fancy to do that, then I don't need nor do I want the damn thing." He gripped Richard's extended hand with both of his large worn hands and shook it.

"How did you know where to find us?" I asked.

"'knew if that horse was hurt Richard would be comin' out the shortest way." Kenneth Moorman said. "This is the shortest way." He released Richard's hand and walked to the back of the trailer.

Richard and I followed him.

He swung the back gates of the trailer open. "'brought the big trailer 'case we needed extra room." He said.

Richard led Harley into the trailer and tied him to the front top left rail. I followed with the black and tied her to the front top right rail. As I fastened the dividing gate behind Harley and the black, Richard coaxed Whiskey into the trailer and tied him to the center of the dividing gate.

"'tore hell out of it. Didn't he?" Kenneth Moorman said as he examined the long deep laceration which ended in a deep gouge just above Whiskey's knee on his left hind leg. "'don't think he tore any ligament though." He said thoughtfully. "Well, let's go. Doc's waitin' for him."

Richard stepped out of the trailer. He and Kenneth Moorman fastened the back gates of the trailer.

Kenneth Moorman walked to the truck along the left side of the trailer. Richard and I walked to it along the right side of the trailer.

As he slid under the padded steering wheel Kenneth Moorman said. "Climb in, boys."

Richard smiled and winked at me as he held the door open for me to get into the cab first. I smiled and slid into the cab. Richard patted his thighs and Jeepers leaped into his lap. Richard pulled the truck door closed.

To Kenneth Moorman and his generation Richard and I, our generation, though in our fifties now, were and would always be 'the boys'; being regarded by men like Kenneth Moorman as 'his boys' was not a bad thing!

As Kenneth Moorman drove back along the path he had bulldozed through the snow to reach us I wondered. Would we have made it out with Whiskey if he had not done so? Probably, because most horses do what you ask of them. And even when you ask a hard thing a good horse like Harley seldom fails you.

8.

The cattle, our cattle, strung out before me as they marched towards the tall sand hill and its steep trail which led to the windmill. I stared east and searched for the fleeing shadow which had flown passed me. If it was a cow it had refused to join our herd. I heard the red roan and glanced at the horse and its rider.

"She had the mark." Richard said as he urged the red roan into a steady trot back down the sloughs.

"'can't be!" I argued, turning the black and letting her quick trot up alongside of the red roan. "She'd have to be pushing thirty to be one of the Captain's old horns."

Richard shrugged and spurred the red roan into an easy gallop. The black changed leads to find her gallop. As she did Richard called. "There! Ahead."

I saw Richard point. I saw something flash ahead of us, the dying sunset's last rays dancing off of what might be thin sinewy flanks and I saw the red roan explode forward after it.

I gave the black her head and before my spurs touched her belly she was racing after Richard and the red roan.

White's Creek appeared out of the darkness, water splashed hard and high from the deep deer pool; once from something I could not see and then from beneath the red roan which had thundered into the pool in full stride.

"Where?" I yelled.

The red roan had its ears pinned back and was swimming with determination for the far side of the deep deer pool. The angry horse was committed to overtake its prey.

Richard pointed at the thick salt cedars at the far side of the pool. "There!"

The black had her ears up. Alert. I urged her across White's Creek and as she surged up the loose slope I saw the cedars move and movement flash through them.

"Did you see it?" I cried.

But the black shot into the cedars in pursuit before I could know if Richard answered. I heard the red roan galloping fast along the edge of the slough nearest the river. I reasoned to take the black to the inside of the cedars and into the slough. In that way whatever we were pursuing would either exit the heavy salt cedars and cross the berm to the river in front of Richard and the red roan or emerge in front of the black and me. Unless it managed somehow to double back through the cedars which I could not imagine it doing because all of us were now running or riding in a full out dash to either escape or capture.

The black flew out of the cedars and into the slough with her ears at full alert, her neck stretched forward and her legs flashing like lightning beneath her.

I gasped for breath and strained to see through my tears which were caused by the wind from the mad speed of the black driving against my face. I saw…I saw…nothing!

But I heard…something! A bellow? A cry? I was not certain of what I was hearing until I heard the red roan's full throated cry of challenge across the thick salt cedars at the edge of the river.

I turned the black back into the cedars without slowing her. She crashed through them and onto the berm at the river's edge. I reined in, hard. The black sat down, her hind legs sliding across the loose sand of the berm and her front legs stiff, extended, and plowing deep into the loose soil. She slid to the very edge, only inches from dropping down the eight feet of the side of the berm and into the quicksand.

The red roan reared and pawed at the night now upon Richard and me, the sunset having finally evaporated. Richard struggled to stay seated in his saddle. He soothed and steadied the red roan.

"Did you see her?" I cried. "Where'd she go?" I stared at the trackless darkness of the river bed.

Richard spoke slowly, softly. "I saw her."

"Where'd she go?" I asked again.

"Into the river." Richard said, his voice faint, fleeting.

"Where?" I stared at the wide bottomless quicksand bog below the berm.

"Right here." Richard whispered.

I eased the black up to the still excited red roan. The horses rubbed their necks together in greeting, the sweat and foam from their all out sprint mixing and dripping down to the sandy ground.

"I don't see a track one in the quicksand. She could not have crossed that much quicksand without leaving a track." I argued as I scoured the quicksand for any sign or mark. "Dammit! Nothing could have crossed that quicksand without leaving some sign!" I continued to argue until I raised my head and stared into Richard's clear eyes.

"'didn't." Richard said. "She went into the river." He said again, slowly. "'not across it."

Richard and I stared into each other's eyes.

"But…" I began to protest, then grew silent.

Richard stared into the darkness above the river. The moon was coming up and the sour milk white of the salt deposits on the river were beginning to glow.

I looked up and down the river, staring with Richard at the wide uninterrupted and uninhabited expanse of the river. I saw nothing!

I felt the red roan turn and the black ease up beside him as they turned away and began the long walk home.

There is a place, a plane, a space where the natural merges with the spiritual. Because it becomes something not discoverable, not definable, it does not form a part of our physical world. Or does it? Have we catalogued all that exists? Is our knowledge of what exists within nature and spirit, and that plain where they collide, so complete that there nothing remains to be discovered?

The Comanche knew this was not so. They knew this place not knowable by sight or sound or touch or smell or feel or taste. They knew it by their faith in their intuitive blood relationship with the natural world. That intuition reasoned such space must exist and the Comanche called it sky and wind and earth and fire and rain as these played with the physical word of men, and that because men could not control the sky or the wind or the earth or the fire or the rain all things were possible within this realm where nature and spirit merged. The Comanche worshipped this place of spirit and nature without feeling any need to explain or define it.

9.

"Hey!" I called as I walked into the east end of the barn. I received no answer. "Hey! Richard." I called again. Then I saw him.

He sat in Sammy's and Aztec's stall. Old Az' lay on his side. His head was in Richard's lap. Richard stroked his muzzle and spoke gently to his old friend each time a spasm racked the great black horse.

Sammy stood in front of Richard. He held his face close to his fallen comrade. Sammy and Aztec had been stalled together for eighteen years, all of Sammy's life since he had been weaned from his mother. The paint horse seemed to realize he was losing his lifelong companion and he whinnied his heartfelt plea to get up to his dieing friend and true to his good heart Az' tried to rise. Another spasm, more savage than the others, punished him for his fealty. Richard stroked his shoulder. "Easy. Easy." He soothed. "Sshsh. Sammy." The paint's sky blue eye and dark brown eye searched Richard's face as if seeking to understand why Richard was scolding him.

Richard looked up at me and a sad sickness shown from his eyes. "Bring me my rifle." He murmured.

"Can't you get him up? We can haul him to the vet." I asked.

Richard shook his head.

"I can call Doc. He'll come." I offered.

Again Richard shook his head. "No. He's down to stay. Never been down before and he wouldn't be down now if he had it left in him to get up." The horse trembled again. "He's hurtin'. Bring me the Winchester." Richard said.

I hesitated. It would be a hard thing for Richard to shoot this horse. I had no desire to do so and I wished less for Richard to.

The horse's body shook violently.

"I don't think he will be hurting for long." I said.

"'don't matter how long it is. He's hurtin' and he counts on me not to let him hurt. Now bring me the damn rifle." Richard commanded.

I lifted the .30-.30 off of the horns which served as its rack above the commode in the separate bathroom we had built in the barn. As I pushed back through the gate of the front stall I saw Jeepers sitting against the water tub in Sammy's and Aztec's stall. His head was down, the angry scar from his battle with the boar was still visible along his side and his torn ear lay splayed apart against his stringy hair, but his eyes were focused upon old Az'. He had spent the winter in Sammy and Az's stall. On the coldest nights he had huddled in the remnants of their hay beneath their lowered heads as they slept standing and he had drawn warmth from their steady exhalations. He, too, knew this was wrong and he was wary and attuned to each movement of the old black horse that lay dying in the stall.

"'want me to do it?" I asked Richard.

He shook his head and said, "No." He reached for the rifle and said, "Go get the big tractor. Bring it around to the outside. I'll open the panels for you."

I released the rifle, nodded and moved away quickly. I climbed into the cab of the Kubota. As I turned the key to heat the diesel engine's cylinders I heard the Winchester thunder and echo underneath the barn followed by two cries, one a high wail, wolf like, the other a low rumbling groan. I did not wait for the heat indicator to go off. I switched the key full to the right and let the rattle of the diesel engine as it started still cold drown out the cries from the barn.

I opened the gate which led to the field and the forsaken old orchard. I drove the tractor through the gate, turned it, aimed it at the blow sand stacked three feet high against the catch pen fence, revved the engine to 2200 rpm, lowered the bucket of the front end loader until it sat level with the bottom of the sand dune, released the clutch and slammed the bucket up to its hilt in the loose sand. I shifted to neutral, pulled down on the hydraulic lever and listened to the tractor groan as it lifted the heavy load of sand.

With the sand filled bucket for ballast I drove back through the gate and turned and drove to the back of Sammy's and Aztec's stall. Richard stood beside the steel panel he had swung back to let the tractor into the stall. He held the Winchester in the crook of his right arm. He nodded his agreement at using the sand as a counterweight to Az's heavy body which lay on its side at the far end of the stall underneath the overhang of the barn. Sammy stood in the first stall which was completely covered by the barn. He hung his head over the gate between that stall and his and Aztec's stall and stared down at the body of the black gelding. Jeepers sat in front of the dead horse's head.

I shifted the tractor into first gear, locked the break on the right rear tire and spun the tractor around. I backed to the dead horse, lowered the hay spike until it rested above the body, shifted the tractor to neutral and idled the engine. As I climbed from the cab Richard carried a long heavy logging chain into the stall. He handed me the rifle and I set it in the cab of the tractor. Together Richard and I worked the heavy chain beneath the corpse. We looped it around the front of its shoulders, around its midsection and around its flanks. I wrapped each end of the chain around the top of the spike where it attached to the center pivot bar of the power lift of the tractor and locked the hook on each end of the chain into the other part of the chain.

"Go easy." Richard said.

"Where?" I asked.

"The Captain's old orchard." Richard said. "Be a good place. 'won't be plowing over him there."

I nodded, climbed back into the cab of the tractor, revved the engine and raised the hay spike. Slowly the corpse rose free of the ground. I shifted into first gear and eased the tractor out of the stall. As I steered the tractor through the gate I looked back. Richard was holding the dead horse's head in his arms, preventing it from dragging on the ground. Jeepers walked behind Richard with his head down. I looked away and steered for the orchard.

We unchained the corpse at a spot shaded by the last two remaining pear trees. Richard used the tractor and excavated a large deep whole just next to the body. Jeepers and I stood beneath the pear trees and watched. When Richard throttled down to put the tractor in reverse and back up out of the hole with a load of dirt we would hear Sammy whinnying at the barn. Richard would throttle up, drown out Sammy's whinnying, back out of the whole, dump the bucket of dirt and return to the whole. For two hours the tractor rolled down into the hole, filled the bucket, lifted it, backed out of the hole and dumped the dirt. At last Richard was satisfied with the depth of the hole. He dumped his final bucket of dirt, shifted the tractor to neutral, and climbed down.

The three of us, Richard, Jeepers and I stood next to the dead horse. Richard had dug the hole where Az's back faced it. In that way it allowed Richard and I to lift Az's stiffening legs and roll him into the hole. The corpse tumbled into the deep hole. Sand and dirt cascaded into the hole with the body which had landed on its feet and crumpled its legs beneath it. Az's head lay torqued upwards by the weight of the heavy body forcing it against the east wall of the grave.

I slid down into the grave and eased Az's head down and between his front legs. I looked up. Richard nodded, extended his hand down to me and pulled me up out of the grave. He walked back to the tractor, climbed into the cab and filled the grave, building a large rectangular mound of dirt atop it. Jeepers and I retreated back beneath the pear trees.

Richard and I had eaten without speaking, listening to Sammy's whinnying slowly subside. Richard leaned against the front stall, sitting on a five gallon bucket and dozing. I sat in a canvas deck chair and stared at the leavings of another sunset.

Jeepers' high pitched battle cry startled us both. It angered Richard. He picked up the .30-.30 and went around the corner of the barn. I followed him.

Two coyotes stood in the field just beyond the pear trees. Jeepers was perched atop Az's grave, teeth bared, screeching a warning at them. Richard raised the rifle to his shoulder.

"Jeepers is seventy yards. The coyotes are better than a hundred." I advised him.

Richard steadied his breathing, felt for the trigger and found it.

I tried to read the probable trajectory of the bullet by the angle of the barrel of the gun, but I was too close to triangulate the shot. "Not the dog!" I cried just as the Winchester discharged.

The coyote nearest Richard and I flipped backwards, twisted twice and lay still. The other coyote raced away with Jeepers pursuing it, cursing barks flying from the little dog, until Richard whistled Jeepers back. The little dog returned to his perch atop the grave.

Richard returned to the barn. "No sleep tonight." He said as he walked passed me. "But, by God, Jeepers is right. There will be no horse meat for those skulking coyotes this night."

I watched him enter the barn and return carrying the rifle in the crook of his right arm, a box of cartridges in his right hand and a canvas lawn chair with his left hand. He walked to the grave and Jeepers, unfolded his chair, set it atop the grave, sat down in it and laid the rifle across his lap.

I walked to my truck and lifted the .223 Ruger Mini-14 from the rack above the back of the seat. I dropped the five shot clip on the seat, dug in my ammunition pouch until I found the thirty shot clip stamped "For Government Use Only", pulled it out and slapped it into the bottom of the receiver. I would chamber a shell when I, too, was seated on Aztec's grave. I retrieved another folded canvas chair from the barn and marched to the grave to join Richard and Jeepers in their long quiet vigil atop their fallen friend.

Richard grieved not for horse, not that in distant eons evolutionary extinction might eventually eliminate horse as a species, not whether horse had been chosen for immortality above all the other species. Richard longed to again hear the thunder of Aztec's hooves thrown against the earth at a gallop and in pursuit, to once more feel Aztec's strong sinewy muscles stretched to their fullest beneath his groomed hide as he overtook and captured a fleeing wheat pasture steer and to acknowledge to Aztec the sweet sharing of spirit Richard had known with this horse whose heart was big and strong and true.

10.

I saddled the black without speaking to Richard. The dream, last night's and a hundred other nights' dream, plagued me, made me melancholy and pushed me to seek solitude to return that dream to its place beneath its shroud of abstinence.

The dream had begun, and continued for many years, as sweet reunion. She and I would meet. By accident or intent, it did not matter. In Austin at the Driskill, San Antonio along the river or in the plaza in Santa Fe, place did not matter. At breakfast or at dinner, time did not matter. None of this would be important because she and I would fall comfortably back into step with one another whenever, wherever and however we met again and we would stay in step for the rest of our lives.

I sought the dream and the dream filled me with hope because the dream let me believe that hope still to be possible of fulfillment. That dream stayed, and came when I called upon it, for a long time.

Until time spilled over my hope and replaced it with anger and resentment of time itself. "Why? Why must time pass? How much must it pass before she and I can be again? How much? And who is to say this or this or this is enough...time?" The meeting now was a confrontation, a confrontation which I could not control and which I was afraid to interpret. "Was it reunion or disunion? Was it now only or forever?" And this dream imposed itself onto the first dream for several years.

But now as if drawn from an opium pipe another dream comes upon me unbidden, relentless and cutting, bringing with it tenebrous death and it is always the same. "I am dead, dead, dead! Before I see her again! Before I speak to her again!" This is the dream now. And I fear it: its immediacy, its reality, its truth---its infinity and its nothingness!

It was this dream I wanted to ride away, alone. But Richard was saddling a horse, too. He intended to ride with me. I glanced over and saw he was saddling Sammy, his old paint.

"'still hung over?" Richard asked.

I shrugged and silently laced the latigo in and out of the cinch ring.

Richard tightened his cinch and said. "Only two things to do for a hangover: Keep drinking or wear it out."

I did not answer him. I struggled to mount the black, had to bounce twice, but managed to pull myself up and into Boss' saddle. I lifted the reins from the black's neck. The black turned away from the round pen and started for the gate which opened onto the dirt road.

Richard swung up and onto his old paint in one smooth easy movement and followed me onto the road and north to the river.

The black found sure footing in the sandy road. She struck an easy lope. The paint matched her stride, but he stayed half a horse length behind and to her right. He had followed Aztec for years. He was content to follow the black. Jeepers trotted behind Sammy.

My thoughts returned to the dream, rocked in and out of focus, coming and going with the black's steady rhythm.

Did she love me? Did she understand that I saw her as a part of my life as much as I saw myself as a part of that life? That I did this intuitively and to do so was as natural to my self as light is natural to morning, as necessary for me as light is necessary for the morning, and as irreplaceable to my psyche as light must be irreplaceable to each dawn? Or, for her, had I just become troublesome, a discomfort best eased by abolition?

This dilemma is something I have turned over in my mind's eye so many times I can no longer find a way to turn it so that I can see it. Has it blinded me? Or did I so truly not know her as she was that my ignorance distorted her beyond any recognition?

I can remember the place, the rocks beneath the tables, the tables beneath the green awning and the green awning beneath the rain cleared skies. Skies which had darkened into a black mat upon which a thousand stars had danced. But I can not remember what we ate that last evening. Time has stolen some of the details from my memory. And time has stolen the chance we had to share a history.

Richard and I reached the decaying old house and the still sturdy rock dugout. I slowed the black to a walk. Richard moved the paint ahead, stopped him, swung down and opened the gate to the river pasture. As Jeepers scurried passed I turned the black through the gate and without waiting for Richard to close the gate I pushed the black into a trot, passed the rock water trough and the windmill and the top lot and reined her right between the two ruts which were the pasture road to the river and returned to my thoughts.

Our histories have not merged again, and what I struggle now to accept is that they will not. While each of us will create our own history, time forces this upon each of us; together she and I shall create no further historical record beyond that February farewell. And this is so, even though and despite my dream and she and I may meet again, on one or a hundred unprovoked occasions or none at all, may even visit and talk and smile at each other. But that, if it happens, will be each one's independent and momentary notation in the coming and going of life, just an accidental aside, and not a marked historical event in our lives. It shall never again be that mutual history of common spirit I remember and believe we shared.

I long for the time that shared common spirit was our history, the time when she was my memory, the time when she was mine to think of, the time I never imagined would end because I had never held her in my arms, only in my heart. No longer can I rest my heart in thoughts of her. With her last words she took this time from me and all hopes of rest from my heart. And she took with her my ability to believe and the energy to direct my dreams. Now my dreams haunt me.

I heard the paint blow out his breath as Richard slowed him from overtaking the black and me. I guided the black onto the ridge above the twisted river field. Now we moved toward the setting sun. Again I let the black go as she wished and returned to my sad revelry.

Once, at least once, I want to taste the sweetness and feel, really feel, the kind of wetness that comes from someone in love with me loving me, with me. See me in her eyes. See my face reflected more truly there than I could ever see it in the finest mirror made with the purest glass the master glassblower could breathe life into.

Richard turned the paint out onto the highest point of the ridge and stopped him. The black stopped, turned and retreated to stand beside the paint. Jeepers sat between the horses. Richard stared across the winter oats of the river field and out onto the river.

I looked at the side of Richard's face and said. "Just once! Just once I want to be that center of someone's life. To be making love to her and to know each sound, each touch, each movement she will make before she makes it. I want to know that feeling! Don't you?"

Richard sat silent.

"Don't you?" I demanded.

Richard straightened on his saddle, stretched his sore back, stared at the river and said. "I want, at least once, to sit here on this very spot and look out at that river." He nodded at the red and white dry river's bed. "I want to do that sitting on the best horse I can train and understand that woman you want." Richard turned his head, looked at me, then turned back to look at the river.

We sat on our horses on the high point above the river field. I could see twenty miles or more in any direction and I could look back into my life twenty plus years and see her, hear her voice and remember what she said to me.

"Someday I will tell you something. Those were the last words she spoke to me." It was as if she had vanished, had been extinguished by some force of nature. But I knew she had not and I had struggled with that knowledge almost daily. I remembered a small graveyard on a cold windy promontory surrounded by a dozen black bred Morgan horses and in my mind's eye I saw that beautifully good young woman standing just before and beside me in that graveyard, her childlike face bent a little forward yielding to cold blasts of wind, her hands driven deep into the pockets of the black cashmere coat she wore to ward away that wind, and my dream, my longing had come together into focus in the elegant sleek coat clad course of the small of her back. Not in the black tailored fabric of her coat as it squared straight across her strong shoulders and not in its softness as it swept itself against her sides, but there in the small of her back, trapped between the concaves formed above each of her small hips and the quiet outflow of her buttocks. Just there, just in the soft seldom seen small of her back! There all the shrouded, disguised, deceiving shadows of my dream withdrew and I knew. I knew! I reached, just to touch her elbow to tell her I knew, and she flinched and in flinching drove away my dream, my knowing, my love.

"She is a love not dead for me." I spoke to the dry salt river. "But she is a love long disappeared in my life." Tears danced into my eyes. I blinked them away. "That is the cruelest love of all."

The quiet coming night began to envelope us. The horses blew through their noses and shuffled their feet, weary of their long stand upon the high hill. Jeepers yawned.

"And maybe it is the strongest love of all." Richard said to the fading redness of the sunset upon the darkening river. "If she cared as you believe she cared that took a great deal of strength. That kind of strength you only find deep inside of you."

I sighed. "I know."

"No." Richard said. "No. You don't." Richard turned and faced me. "You can't. You're not that deep."

I opened my mouth to protest, to defend my righteousness in how I felt about this. Before I could do so the world spun, Boss' saddle disappeared from beneath me and I lay gasping for breath amidst the sage brush, side oats gramma grass and bear grass spears.

"Damn horse." I sputtered, caught my breath and cursed. "Damn horse! Damn this horse!" I lifted my knees by using my spurs to climb my boots free of the grip the ground seemed to hold upon them. "Oh!" I groaned. "Damn horse has done it to me again, Richard."

Richard's shoulders shook. Laughter, soft and sweet and truly enjoyed, tumbled down from the hill and echoed away across the dry river. Richard shook his head and continued to laugh. "'looked to me like you fell off." He laughed harder.

"Again?"

"Again."

"If I somehow manage to get up, what do I do now?" I groaned. I forced my elbows into the ground beneath me and raised myself onto them. Jeepers licked my cheek.

Richard's shoulders continued to shake from his not fully suppressed laughter. He looked away from me and to the river.

"Well, goddammit! Are you thinking or have you gone to sleep with your eyes open?"

Richard slowly formed his words. "Well." He stopped.

I glared at him. "Well what?"

Richard chewed on his bottom lip. "If you're askin' me." He stopped again.

"Dammit! I just asked you! Didn't I?"

Richard pushed his hat back on his head.

I dropped my chin onto my chest and waited, wondering if Richard would bestow some epiphany as to life and its meaning or just mumble another of his inaudible and nonsensical mundane nesses.

Richard spoke slowly. He always spoke slowly. "You get back on the horse."

"Again?"

Richard nodded and said. "Again."

"But I thought you said last time if she wasn't passed this she probably never would be passed it." I protested.

Richard nodded again and said. "Probably not."

I exploded. "Goddammit! What's the goddamn purpose of that? What's the goddamn purpose of any of it?" I cried.

Richard shrugged and laughed. "No particular purpose I guess." He extended his hand down to me and pulled me to my feet and said. "It's just what you do when you're trainin' horses and you fall off your horse."

"Damn this horse and damn you." I tried to curse, but I gave up and laughed, too, as I struggled to remount. I realized Richard knew me too well. Maybe she had also?

11.

Winter left swiftly that year. The second day of April Richard and I stood beneath the open east end of the barn. I held Boss's saddle and propped it against my left hip. I held a snaffle bit bridle in my right hand. Richard held his Terry Brewer saddle in his right hand. He had a hackamore with braided reins draped over his left shoulder. The two orphan black calves, the smallest orphaned by chance, by his mother's death and the largest orphaned by choice, rejected by his mother, sat one each side of Jeepers at the east end of the barn, also.

Richard and I had left the red roan and the black filly standing in the round pen where we had galloped them for almost half an hour and we had fled to the barn before the rainstorm showered us. The red roan and the black filly chased each other, revived and invigorated by the cool wet air left behind from the passing storm.

Richard and I stared above the serrated tops of the rough cut quarter rounds which made up the walls of the round pen.

Two rainbows carved great ellipses across the eastern sky, one atop the other. Two ends to the rainbows finding ground just before the last sand hills before the river on the north and the other two ends finding their roots in the tall Indian and switch grass of the Conservation, Restoration and Preservation field to the south. Orange, yellow, green, blue, purple, violet equalized streamers bent across the white white backside of the departing rain storm. Each rainbow was pure of color, form and presentation. Each color was true and bright and vivid as if lifted from some sky painter's pallet. No blemish stained their composition. No flaw faulted their lines. No impurity discolored their brilliance.

They were perfect and they were real. And yet they were unattainable. No quest, however impassioned and long persevered, could come even one step closer to them than Richard and I were at that moment. No eye could see them better than we saw them. No mind could know them more intimately than we knew them in that moment.

Epilogue

The years are beginning to pass Richard and me by at an accelerating rate. We have held to the place and the horses, and by holding on to the place and the horses we have held on to each other.

Richard continues to measure time by the horses he has trained---the bad ones, the good ones and the great ones. Richard is one of the few remaining horsemen of these short grass prairies who know a horse by its gait, its breathing and its will to give and its heart to endure. In a generation or two no such horsemen will remain, partly because they have left behind too few offspring to continue their genetics and partly because their skills are no longer thought necessary or important, but mostly because so few understand and, therefore, value the intuitive kindred spirit these riding men share with their horses.

I measure time by the black and the foals she throws. I am riding one now, a black filly, the image of her dam. And, each once and awhile, I saddle the black. She is older now and not as quick. Thus, I do not fear falling off as I did that first winter with her. But early last spring, for no reason other than possibly to remind me who was still in control, she went left when I was going right. Lying on my back in a clump of sagebrush, Richard sitting on a young colt and shaking his head and laughing, and the black staring big-eyed at me I swore. "Richard. I will never name this damn horse."

And I have not named her. And I will not. For me she is the black and Richard is my brother who trains horses. That is enough.